WHAT'S YOUR DREAM?

ARIANA GOLD

Huntington City Township
Public Library
255 West Park Drive
Huntington, IN 46750
www.huntingtonpub.lib.in.us

Sports Illustrated Kids What's Your Dream books
are published by Stone Arch Books

A Capstone Imprint

1710 Roe Crest Drive
North Mankato, Minnesota 56003
www.mycapstone.com

Library of Congress Cataloging-in-Publication Data is available
on the Library of Congress website.

ISBN: 978-1-4965-3442-2 (library binding)
ISBN: 978-1-4965-3446-0 (paperback)
ISBN: 978-1-4965-3450-7 (eBook pdf)

Designer: Russell Griesmer

Editor: Nate LeBoutillier

Production Specialist: Kathy McColley

Photo Credits:
Design Elements: Shutterstock

Printed and bound in the USA
009657F16

WHAT'S YOUR DREAM?

ARIANA GOLD

BY JOELLE WISLER

STONE ARCH BOOKS
a capstone imprint

CHAPTER ONE

Ariana Gold stepped onto the ice, and the crowd went crazy.

Go Ariana! We love you, Ari! Your mom would be proud, Ariana!

They don't even know me, Ariana thought. The ice knew her, however, and it welcomed the blades of her skates like an old friend.

Ariana realized many people loved her because of her mother, Daisy. When Daisy won the silver medal at the Olympics, America cried real tears of pride for the redheaded beauty, but also disappointment. The gold medal had been just a tenth of a point away.

With her head of red curls and her powerful jumps, Ariana looked just like her mother. She was also chasing her mother's ice skating dreams. Her parents had made "Gold" her middle name, after all.

Ariana could remember her first day at the skating rink. She was just three years old. Each time her legs had splayed out from under her and she fell over, her dad had scooped her up. "You'll be a champ like your mom someday," he said. "You'll see."

Before she could become a champion like her mom, Ariana had to get herself to the Junior World Championships. She was the last of the six finalists to do the free skate portion of her program. She would need every point. At just thirteen years of age, Ariana was by far the youngest girl on her team. She was mostly inexperienced when it came to competitions.

Right before the music started, Ariana glanced up at her dad's usual spot near the judges. The cheering crowd looked like a smiling mouth. The open spot where her dad should have been, however, was like a missing tooth that left an embarrassing hole.

Where is he? Ariana thought.

Her dad, Jack, spent nearly all of his time working so that Ariana could follow their Olympic skating dream. He had never missed a competition before. Not once.

Jack had struggled ever since Daisy died, soon after Ariana was born. Daisy and her skating had been Jack's entire life. Then he was suddenly left alone with a crying baby. He had done the best he could. He had given Ariana love and hours of ice time. But Jack relied on Ariana to act more like a grown-up than most thirteen-year-old girls.

Ariana often came home exhausted. Her days were long with school and hours of ice time perfecting her turns and jumps. Sometimes, she tried to talk to him about how tired she was. But her dad would shake his head, not wanting to listen.

"If you work hard enough, all of our dreams will come true," he would say.

She knew how important it was to him that she fill her mother's skates. He had given up a lot for her. Now she wondered where he could be if he hadn't spent all his time and energy and money on her. Or if he'd put at least a little more of all of that toward himself.

The beginning notes of her song started to play, so Ariana forced herself to focus on her routine. She reached for her neck to feel the weight of her mom's necklace. It was a medallion with a picture of a golden skater twirling. It held all of her luck and had been with her for every performance. On the back were the engraved words, *Give it all to the ice.* As the metal cooled her fingers, she brushed away thoughts of her missing father.

Ariana started out with her spin combinations. Her skirt floated around her, highlighting the nuance of her every move. At just over five feet tall, she was small and couldn't match the long-limbed gracefulness of her taller peers. The magic happened when she brought in her jumps. Ariana didn't just jump. She flew.

Coach Carly had urged her to try to impress the judges right out of the gate. With that in mind, Ariana started to pick up speed, the ice smooth and solid under her skates. She loved the feeling of her muscles as they anticipated the next actions. She did her step sequence and then flew into the first of her spins. Her hand caught her heel in a graceful arc.

As Ariana approached her jump combination, she felt a fierceness that came from somewhere inside of her. The music swelled. She readied for the familiar feeling of flying across the smooth surface.

She hit the spot where she knew she needed to start skating the backward crosscut motions. This would prepare her for the starting position of her double lutz.

She pulled her left arm up in front of her, bent her left knee, and leapt. As the world spun, she felt like she had started the jump too fast. But she checked her speed and landed on her right leg without a single bobble.

There wasn't a moment to think before she was driving her toe pick into the ice and whipping her body into a double toe loop. The cheers of the crowd lifted the roof as she met the ice. Ariana had dreams of skating every night, but they were never as good as the real thing.

She willed herself to avoid searching out her dad in the stands. *He's there by now,* she thought. *He's never missed a competition.*

Trying to concentrate on the next section of her routine, she went inside herself again. The final jump was coming.

Ariana knew she had a choice now. She could stick with her double loop, or she could triple it.

Her friend, Sasha, had gotten a 5.8 with a clean, if not overly hard, program. If Ariana went with the double, Sasha would beat her. If she landed the triple and kept her routine clean, Ariana would be guaranteed the win and the last spot on the team going to Worlds. But she had never landed a triple in competition before, and Coach Carly would be angry if she even tried. She had said Ariana wasn't ready for the triple loop yet. If she tried the triple and fell, Ariana would blow her chances completely.

All of these thoughts were fluttering through Ariana's mind as she finished the last of her smaller spins and footwork. Even she didn't know what she was going to do until she rounded the last turn and started to pick up speed.

Ariana could feel her coach's eyes on her. Coach Carly knew that Ariana was going too fast now for just a double. For a moment, Ariana doubted the notion she was having.

As the takeoff spot on the ice approached, she made her final decision.

She dug her skate into the ice, like she had thousands of times. Her body prepared for takeoff. Many in the crowd seemed to realize what she was planning to do and went silent.

Time stopped.

Ariana spun in the air. She thought she could feel the crowd counting with her . . . *one* . . . *two* . . . *three revolutions*. And then her left foot landed, touching down slightly wrong. A gasp came from the stands.

She should have landed on the inside edge of her skate, but she hit the outside edge. Ariana could read the tiniest angles with the movements of her ankles. She knew she had to correct, and the thrill of the jump was thrown from her brain.

It took every single ounce of calf and ankle strength that she had, but she pulled herself upright. She saved the landing. Barely.

The crowd roared. Ariana snuck a peek at the judges, and they were grinning. One of the men was shaking his head as if he couldn't believe his eyes.

Ariana had done it. She knew she had.

She looked over into the stands, hoping to see her dad standing up and cheering his head off.

But he wasn't there.

CHAPTER TWO

Ariana sat silently in the backseat of the car while Sasha chattered like a squirrel.

"Can you believe it?" Sasha said. "We're both going to Junior Worlds. The hard work is finally paying off."

"Yeah," said Ariana. She clutched the gold medal in her fist. Her fingers had turned red, white, and angry from the pressure. She had won. She was going to Junior Worlds as the youngest girl in the competition. She should've been thrilled.

Jenny, one of their teammates, would've been thrilled to be in Ariana's place. Instead, Jenny had been crying in the locker room afterward. It was

Jenny's last chance to qualify for the Junior Worlds, and Ariana had taken her spot, putting Jenny in the alternate position.

Ariana had felt Jenny's mom staring daggers at her as she walked out of the arena.

Sasha looked over at Ariana. "Are you okay, Ari?"

Though the girls competed against each other, there had never been any hard feelings between the two of them. This wasn't the case with Jenny, who always hated to lose, especially to Ariana because she was so young.

"I'm fine," said Ariana. "Just tired, I guess." She looked out the window and tried to ignore the sour feeling in her stomach. She couldn't stop thinking about her dad.

Ariana spied Mrs. Roland in the rearview mirror, her brows knitted together. Sasha's *two* parents were in the car. Both of whom had been cheering their daughter on at the competition. Both of whom had looked sympathetically at Ariana when they offered her a ride back home to Colorado Springs.

For months, Ariana's dad had struggled to keep both of his jobs so that Ariana could skate double practices and have a professional coach. Ariana had offered again and again to cut the time she spent at the arena. It would save them a lot of money. But her dad always refused, saying, "You need that time on the ice, my golden girl."

Ariana's whole life was ice. Usually she didn't mind. She loved that she looked like her mom and skated like her mom. She had never known her mom, so it was as if skating was an invisible thread that connected them. And she loved making her dad happy.

Sasha's parents dropped Ariana off at her house. "You call if you need anything, okay sweetie?" said Mrs. Roland.

Ariana forced a smile. "I will," she said.

Even though her dad's car was in the driveway and the house lights were on, the Rolands didn't drive off until they saw Ariana's dad let her in the front door.

"Hey there, golden girl," said Jack, hugging his daughter. He sat down at the kitchen table and cracked open a soda. The newspaper was spread out in front of him, and he had dark circles under his eyes. "So," he said, "how was practice today?"

Ariana couldn't believe it. He had completely forgotten about the competition.

"I, uh . . . it was the competition today, Dad," Ariana said.

The distracted smile he had been wearing dripped off his face like he was some wax sculpture in a heat wave.

Ariana continued, trying to be cheerful now. "Yeah . . . it's, you know, no big deal that you weren't there," she said. "Coach has video and everything."

Ariana plastered a huge fake grin on her face. And then she placed her gold medal on the table like a token. "And, guess what? I landed that triple loop!"

"Oh, Ari," he said. "I'm so sorry." He sighed and rubbed his chin. "I've just been getting my days mixed up."

Ariana couldn't look him in the eye. "Like I said, not a big deal." She started to pick up the dirty dishes in the kitchen, scraping them and then opening the dishwasher. He hadn't even acknowledged the triple. He was acting strange.

Ariana continued, hoping to shake him out of whatever funk he was in, "And, now . . . now I get to go to the Junior Worlds. Our dreams are actually coming true!" Ariana could do cheerful for miles.

Her dad's face went pale. "There's something we need to talk about, Ari-girl."

Ari stopped tidying. His tone was really starting to freak her out. She waited for him to go on.

"Well . . . we've run into some trouble," he said finally.

Ariana sat down next to him at the table. "What is it?" she asked, not knowing if she wanted to hear the answer.

"It's our savings." He reached over and gently rubbed her back, just like he did on those rare nights these days that he remembered to tuck her in. "*Your* savings. From your mom."

"I put most of it into this tech stock . . . " he continued, but Ariana's mind took a leap. She didn't understand anything about stocks, but she knew from the sound of his voice and the look on his face that the money she got from her mom was gone. And that brought up a ton of bad possibilities.

They had relied on Ariana's savings heavily. She knew it had dwindled over the years. Her dad kept saying it would all be worth it in the end. And he often volunteered for overtime so that she could get extra ice time and not dip into the savings as much. She hated that he worked so hard for her, but he always told her it was the most important thing to him. Skating was the most important thing.

"Can I still skate?" Ariana asked.

"I've paid Coach Carly and the rink up until the end of this month."

"But Junior Worlds is in two months."

"If something doesn't change, we won't have the money to send you. I'm really sorry, Ari." He dropped his head into his hands.

"Well, can I tell Coach — "

"Please don't, Ariana," said Jack. "We'll tell Carly *some*thing. I'm just . . . I'm too ashamed right now. And I'm trying to find a way to earn the money back. I am."

Ariana couldn't believe it. All of the hours she spent skating. The time away from friends. The studying until midnight to keep her grades up.

It all meant nothing.

She felt a tightness in her chest and knew she had to get away. She couldn't believe that her dad had lost everything.

All of a sudden she hated him. And then she felt guilty for hating him when he had done everything for her.

What would she tell Coach Carly? What would she tell Sasha and the rest of the girls? Jenny would be happy — she would get Ariana's place on the team. And everyone would find out, eventually. Even without Ariana telling them.

She bolted up from the table and walked toward the kitchen door, not looking at him.

"Ariana, wait," he said.

But she didn't wait. She ran to her room. Sadness, disappointment, and anger bubbled up in her, and she slammed her door. Her breath hitched, and she buried her face in her pillow.

She ripped off her mom's necklace in a sharp jerk, pain stinging the back of her neck. The golden chain broke easily in her fingers. Hot tears flowed down her cheeks. She opened her window and flung the necklace out.

CHAPTER THREE

Ariana had locked the door to her room the night before and ignored her dad's pleas to talk. She cried herself to sleep and awoke the next morning with her brain fogged over and her eyes swollen.

A few more weeks of paid training. What was the point? She knew it would be impossible for him to work hard enough to earn her savings back. This would be the end of her skating career.

She usually went to the rink before her first classes at school. But now she didn't have the heart. She dressed in dark clothes, hoping the shadowy colors would help her sink into the background.

Unfortunately, everyone had heard about the competition.

Walking through the halls, she got pats on the back and shouts of *Way to go, Ariana!* She fell deeper into her misery.

Even her teachers knew about her big win. Her math teacher, Mr. Kopel, pulled her aside as she tried to leave his class. "Everything okay, Ariana?" Mr. Kopel asked.

She fought to keep the tears down. "Yep," she chirped. "Just great!"

Mr. Kopel didn't look convinced. He was easily her favorite teacher. He'd made sure she didn't have big assignments due when she needed to put in extra hours on the ice. He also occasionally set aside time to tutor Ariana after school or on weekends when she needed it. Mr. Kopel and his family always made it to her competitions wearing T-shirts in Ariana's signature gold color to show their support.

It was teachers like Mr. Kopel who kept Ariana afloat in public school. Most girls at her skating level had private tutors. Of course, Ariana and her dad didn't have the money for that.

"You know I'm always here if you need someone to talk to," Mr. Kopel said kindly.

"Yeah, I know. Thanks." To keep from crying again, she bolted out of the math classroom.

Ariana knew she shouldn't miss two practices in a row, so she took her usual bus to the rink after school. Normally, practice was her favorite part of the day. Now she barely even noticed the bright bluebird sky or the season's first snowfall, an event she usually enjoyed. Her world had gone gray.

Coach Carly gave Ariana a hug when she met her on the rink. "Hey," she said. "I'm really proud of you — but we *are* going to talk about that triple."

Ariana saw her coach's eyes twinkle as she spoke, so she knew she wasn't in too much trouble.

"For now," said Coach Carly, "let's get started on some drills."

"I already did them," Ariana said. She hadn't, but she couldn't really imagine putting her body through the intense warm-ups. Her heart wasn't in it, and her legs felt like two broken-off sticks.

"Really?" Carly said. "Didn't the bus just get here? I just saw Sasha still lacing up in back."

"Yeah, really," Ariana said. Her response came off sharper than she'd intended, so she skated away. She wanted to work on jumps. Just jumps. If her days on the ice were numbered, she was going to work on what she was best at.

Coach Carly watched her young prodigy skate off. It wasn't the first time that she hoped Ariana's pride wouldn't get in the way of her skating.

Ariana began circling the rink. She was determined to land a triple axel before she ran out of ice time. The triple axel was the hardest jump that would be attempted at Junior Worlds. Her mom, Daisy, had been the first woman ever to land the triple axel in a competition.

Ariana had worked for months and was still unable to land it. The axel was far harder than the triple loop that Ariana had pulled off in yesterday's competition. The axel began in a forward position and was really three-and-a-half revolutions. Ariana knew she needed more strength, but she felt an irrational determination to do it. If she was going to prove to the world that she could fill her mom's skates, it would be by landing a triple axel. Time was ticking.

Picking up speed, Ariana planned for the best moment to leap. And in *three . . . two . . . one . . .* Ariana planted her left foot, twisting her body like a rubber band to fling herself around. But even before she left the ground, she knew it was all wrong. Her muscles hadn't warmed up enough, and she had too much nervous energy.

She sprung, but too hard. She pulled her body in tight in an attempt to salvage the speed she had built up, but it was too much. She rotated two and a half, three and a half times. Then her legs buckled under her, and she hit the ice hard.

She managed to protect her head, but her right foot landed at an odd and painful angle, twisting her knee.

When Ariana looked up, she saw her coach's angry face.

"What were you thinking?" said Coach Carly. "A triple axel right out of the gate? Really?"

Ariana didn't say anything.

Coach Carly wasn't finished. "And I know you didn't warm up, Ariana," she said. "What has gotten into you today?"

The older girls watched as their coach hollered. Ariana caught Jenny, in particular, smirking before skating into a perfect arabesque. Ariana's pride now hurt as much as her knee did.

Ariana tugged at her braid. "Well, I landed that triple loop in the competition yesterday, and you didn't think I could do it," Ariana said. She couldn't believe she was saying the words as they came out of her mouth.

Her coach's face went even darker. "With that attitude," said Coach Carly, "you have no business being here today." She turned her back to Ariana. "Why don't you go home and come back when you want to take this seriously."

Ariana couldn't believe it.

Coach Carly had never kicked her off the ice before. She clambered awkwardly to her feet and skated off, trying to ignore the twinge of pain in her knee. She slammed the gate without another look behind her.

She tried to hold her chin high as the other girls snickered, but she flinched when she overheard a stray comment.

Well, she is only thirteen. Maybe she's just too immature for real skating.

Ariana could have sworn she recognized the voice. She was certain it was Sasha's.

CHAPTER FOUR

A week went by, and Ariana moved through her life like a kid-shaped robot. She went to school, ate her meals, and skated twice a day, but her joy was gone, just like her mom's necklace. She ate dinner with her dad every night. They sat in silence eating heated-up mac-n-cheese or frozen pizza. The glow of the computer lit her dad's face as he searched the Internet for jobs. He didn't even ask about Ariana's skating.

At practice, Coach Carly punished Ariana with endless strengthening and endurance drills. Ariana's knee was still sore from her fall, and she wasn't allowed to do any jumps at all.

In addition, Ariana had seen Jenny's mom arguing with Coach Carly. This added to Ariana's overall feeling of anxiety. She knew Jenny wanted her spot at Junior Worlds and would do anything to get it. Jenny's parents gave the rink a lot of money, and everyone knew it.

Figure skating felt like a job that Ariana didn't know if she wanted anymore. One day before practice, she caught a glimpse of her own eyes in the mirror as she yanked her fiery hair into a severe ponytail. They looked tired and much older than a thirteen-year-old's.

Later, she etched fresh grooves onto the ice with her skates and tried to remember the excitement she used to feel. She inhaled the frosty air into her lungs and willed it to soothe her mind. But if the ice had once been her best friend, it had abandoned her for happier skaters.

Like Jenny.

Jenny was skating with more determination than ever, and Coach Carly was even working with her on the triple axel. Ariana felt like the triple axel was *her* jump.

More than once, when she felt like the world was against her, Ariana reached up to touch her lucky necklace.

Each time she came away empty-handed. *Maybe that necklace really did hold all of my luck,* she thought.

After hours of skating crossrolls and doing boring lines and basic novice skills, Ariana's legs were spaghetti, and her back ached. But none of it hurt as much as her heart. She still couldn't bring herself to tell Coach Carly that she and her father were out of money. That was, unless her dad came up with a job that probably didn't exist.

While Ariana attempted her millionth Y spin of the night, Sasha skated up to her. "Hey there," Sasha said. "Sorry Coach is being so hard on you."

Ariana knew Sasha had been in the group that had laughed at Ariana the day that Coach Carly sent her home. They hadn't really talked since that day, mostly because Ariana had been avoiding Sasha. She had begun to feel envious that Sasha would get to go to Worlds and she wouldn't.

"So, my mom wanted me to ask if you wanted to share a room at Worlds," said Sasha, fidgeting with the tassels on her purple skirt. "I know your dad can't always get off work for that long, but we need to be there for the whole week."

Oh, I see, thought Ariana. *Sasha's* mom *is making her be nice.* Anger tightened Ariana's chest, and she said, "Actually, I don't need to room with you." She whipped her hair around, her skates slicing the ice. "My dad *will* be there. I have to get back to my drills."

Ariana couldn't see the look on Sasha's face but hoped it looked somehow similar to what Ariana felt on the inside.

Sasha and the other girls at the rink treated Ariana poorly for the rest of the practice. Ariana heard them whispering and felt them looking at her, but she didn't care. Feeling like an outsider was familiar to Ariana, being so much younger. She'd also dealt with jealousy before because she'd always been the first to be able to land the jumps.

After practice, she changed into her street clothes, alone, in the locker room. She tried to convince herself that being alone was better. She would be gone soon, anyway.

That night, Ariana's dad met her at the door. Her legs were so tired that she stumbled up the three brick steps to her house. He stood at the top, a frown blackening his face. A piece of paper flapped in his hands like an angry flag.

"What's up, Dad?" Ariana asked, though she thought she already knew. The paper he held looked just like the form he filled out for her teachers when she needed some extra time getting her homework done. He gave it to the principal when a big competition was coming up.

Ariana had downloaded one of the forms earlier in the week. She filled it out with her dad's name and handed it in. She had been counting on her dad not finding out. She wished for a hole in the ground large enough to swallow her up.

"You know what's up," he said, slapping the form down on the table. "I'm trying my darnedest to figure something out to keep you skating. But this . . . this is not going to help." His voice was angry but his face looked sad.

Guilt curdled in Ariana's guts like spoiled milk. She hunched her back as if that would keep his words from reaching her.

He continued, pacing in front of her now, "Mr. Kopel called because he wanted to know where the upcoming competition was going to be."

Ariana felt downright terrible. *Mr. Kopel is going to hate me,* she thought. *He's been so nice, and now I've let him down.*

"Your teachers are supporting you," her dad said. "I don't want you taking advantage of them like this." He slumped onto the couch like a one hundred-year-old.

"I don't know what to do," he said. "I wish your mother were here."

The words her father spoke weighed on Ariana like heavy stones. "I do, too," she said, finally lifting her head to meet his eyes.

It had always been just the two of them. The hours and hours at the skating rink, the trips all over the country to compete, the homework, the laundry, the meals, the goodnight kisses. They had always been a team. Ariana knew that they both felt like he had let her down when he lost their savings.

"You know," he said, "she would have been proud of you." He patted the spot beside him. "You're just like her."

Ariana sat down beside him, but his comment made her feel even worse. For once, she didn't want to be just like her mom. How could she live up to being America's sweetheart? She wished that just being Ariana was enough. She leaned into him but couldn't find the words to say what she meant.

Later that night, she lay in her bed making a list in her head. She felt like she had let Mr. Kopel down. Coach Carly was mad at her. Sasha probably hated her. Jenny was determined to get her spot on the team. Her dad expected her to be someone she wasn't. How had she disappointed so many people so quickly? She felt very alone.

She couldn't help but think that things would've been different if her mother was alive. Maybe Ariana's skating wouldn't have been so important to her dad if he'd had Daisy around. Maybe skating was more her parents' dream than it was Ariana's. *Maybe,* she thought, *it would be easier to just screw up so bad that nobody would expect anything of me anymore.*

The more she thought about it, the more she realized that the dream she seemed to be losing might not even be hers.

CHAPTER FIVE

"Today, girls," said Coach Carly, smiling at Ariana for the first time in a week, "we're going to be focusing on jumps."

Ariana couldn't help but feel excited. No matter what else was going wrong, jumps were her favorite thing in the world. Whirling through the air, feeling the ice crystals in her lungs, hearing the sharp snap of the perfect landing. Jumps made the troubles in Ariana's world disappear. Jumps freed her from thinking about lost money, competitions, or any of her other problems.

"Okay," Carly said. "Let's warm up!" She clapped her hands.

The sound of skates scraping across the ice competed with the girls' excited voices. Their frozen breath made them look like graceful, colorful, fire-breathing dragons.

Coach Carly seemed to have forgiven Ariana. They would have to talk soon, but not right then. It was time for flying.

The warmups began as Coach Carly started barking out drills. Ariana had always been strong, but she felt like her muscles had new life from all of the increased legwork she had been forced to do over the past week. Her knee no longer twinged. *Maybe all of those leg drills actually helped,* Ariana thought begrudgingly.

The girls went one after another while Coach Carly shouted corrections. *Arms up! Point that toe! You are swans — not ugly ducklings!*

Even Sasha looked over at Ariana and rolled her eyes as they started their millionth line drill and circled back around for backward crosscuts. Crosscuts were how they would enter all of the jumps except the axel. The girls did crosscuts over and over until they were all sweating.

When their muscles were warm and ready to get off the ground, the girls broke off into different groups — those who would work on their triples, which were senior-level skills, and those who were just training to get to the junior level.

Coach Carly had Ariana go first and demonstrate each jump since she was the only one who had consistently landed triples already. Ariana knew the other girls envied her, but she tried not to think about all of that. She thought only of how her legs moved beneath her and how her arms balanced her. She thought of each tiny shift of weight upon the small blade of metal that connected her with the ice.

Double axel, double toe loop, double lutz, each with slightly different entries. They did them all.

Finally Coach Carly said, "Okay Ari, let's see if we can get some more speed here. Let's see a triple like you did in the last competition." She winked at Ariana, providing Ariana with even more evidence that she had been forgiven.

Ariana hadn't practiced many of the other triples lately since she wasn't allowed to jump. And the only triple she'd been thinking about was the triple axel. Ariana paused and dug her toe pick into the ice. "So, Coach," she said, "I was wondering if — "

"You want to work on the axel," Coach Carly said simply. "You think you're ready?"

Ariana was more than ready. If she had to be done skating, she'd bring the memory of doing a triple axel with her when she left. She'd do it for her mom.

"I'm ready," Ariana said. She threw her shoulders back to try to seem bigger and more sure.

"Well, all right then." Coach Carly's breath came out like a puff of smoke. "Let's see what you've got."

Ariana would skate with everything that she had. She *would* land that triple axel. She felt a slight memory of pain in her knee from the last time she tried the axel. But this time would be different.

For the first time since her dad's bad news, Ariana felt like her old self. The passion that she had been missing thrummed through her veins as she circled around to get into position. Her heart raced, and the details of her surroundings came into sharp focus. Jenny's green practice outfit. Carly's black-gloved hands rubbing together. A strand of her own red hair whipping across her face.

Ariana was going to get that triple axel. She picked up speed, faster and faster.

When she hit the right spot in the ice, she planted her left foot on the outside edge of her skate and climbed up into the air with her right foot, twisting her body around. She really felt like she was in the perfect position.

But she didn't have enough height, and she tumbled to the ice. The fall wasn't as bad as before. This time she bounced right up and brushed the shards of ice off of her black skirt.

She tried again. And failed. And again. Her teammates watched her as she fell four, five, six, seven times.

Carly shouted that her right arm was lagging behind. That she was rotating too early. That she needed her arms and legs to work in perfect unison if she hoped to make it through the full three and a half revolutions.

She was sore and tired and was on the verge of giving up when she remembered something. She had watched her mom's Olympic videos thousands of times. She had seen her mother land her own triple axel again and again. Ariana had practiced twirling and jumping for hours in their living room, mimicking her mother's motions.

All of a sudden, she remembered a stray thought that she had once while watching her mother start the jump. She remembered thinking that her mother looked like Superman while taking off because she leapt so far forward instead of up high.

So, during Ariana's eighth attempt, she skated harder and faster. When the time to leap came, she leapt *out* instead of up.

The result was magic.

The outward leap gave her enough time and space to spin three and a half revolutions and land perfectly.

All of the girls clapped and cheered. Ariana hadn't felt that way in weeks. The feeling lasted all throughout practice, where she landed two more triple axels. She celebrated with the other girls as they made their own jumps.

After practice, tired and elated, Ariana was walking toward the locker room when she overheard Sasha talking to Jenny.

"I heard her dad lost all of their money," Sasha said. Her voice was a whisper, but Ariana could still hear it. "She won't be able to go anyway."

They were talking about her! Ariana felt her blood go hot.

Sasha continued, "So even if she does have her triple axel, you'll totally get her spot."

Ariana couldn't believe what she heard. All of her previous joy drained out of her like yarn unraveling.

Sasha squealed, "We're going to have so much fun!" and high-fived Jenny just as Ariana rounded the corner.

The two girls looked up. Guilt smeared their faces.

"You don't deserve my spot," Ariana growled at Jenny.

Jenny glared at Ariana. "This is my last chance, Ariana," Jenny said. "My mom already talked to Coach Carly. If you can't go, I'm taking your spot. I've worked for years for this, and you aren't going to take it away from me."

Ariana balled her hands into fists. Her voice came out low and calm. "You two will never be anything but second and third best," said Ariana. "You'll have to live with yourselves knowing that. I actually feel sorry for you."

Sasha looked like she was about to cry. Jenny stood there dumbfounded until a smirk sparked across her face as she looked past Ariana to the space behind her.

Ariana slowly turned around and saw Coach Carly standing there.

Carly had heard everything Ariana said.

"Go home, Ariana," said Coach Carly, storm clouds in her eyes. "And don't come back to my rink until you can learn how to be a good teammate."

CHAPTER SIX

For an entire week, Ariana's dad didn't know that she wasn't going to skating practice.

Each morning, Ariana awoke and made a show of putting her skates and her practice clothes in her bag. She still rode the early bus, but instead of getting off at the rink, she took it all the way to school. She did her homework in the library until the bell rang and kids began to roll in like a babbling river.

She was a perfect and polite student. She quietly finished her schoolwork, and she caused no trouble. She snuck around school like a spy, scared that someone would talk to her and blow her cover.

She did miss skating.

She missed the squeeze of her skates as she laced them up, and she missed the apple-crisp smell of the frozen air. She missed the slivers of shaved ice that her skates tossed up with each turn. She even missed the rumble of the Zamboni as it smoothed out her canvas. Worst of all, she felt like she'd lost the only connection she'd ever had to her mom.

Her dad had an upcoming interview that could bring in more money. This cheered him. He remembered to tuck her in at bedtime three nights in a row. "If I get the job, maybe they'll let me work overtime," he said on one of those nights. "Then I might be able to pay for some ice time."

Bedtime had always been Ariana's favorite time of day. It was when she could be Ariana the Kid, not Ariana the Future Olympic Gold Medalist. And these days she definitely felt more like Ariana the Kid. Though she missed the Medalist.

"Sure, Dad," Ariana said, avoiding his eyes.

"You don't believe me?" he said, sweeping the hair from her face. "You'll see. We'll get back on that Olympic track. You could go to Worlds next year, maybe."

He looked so hopeful that Ariana didn't have the heart to tell him that she wasn't ever going to skate again.

He surprised her with his next words. "You know, your mom didn't always have it easy, either."

Ariana had never heard this before. As far as she'd been told, her mother had been a star the moment she'd donned a pair of skates. Ariana was always curious to hear of new details about her mom. "What do you mean?" she asked.

He snuggled her closer. "Well, when she was twelve, she had a major growth spurt," he said.

"Really?" Ariana had heard of this happening. Growth spurts had ruined skaters' careers before.

"Yeah," he said. "She had to relearn all of her jumps again with her new, longer legs."

Ariana couldn't imagine having to start over. The knowledge that her mom had struggled too made Ariana feel closer to her, somehow. Like Daisy hadn't been perfect, either.

"Good thing it looks like you're going to be a shrimp!" He ruffled Ariana's hair and gave her a kiss on the forehead.

Ariana squeezed his hand.

"G'night, kiddo," he said. "You gotta get up and work on that axel!"

"G'night, Dad."

Ariana fell asleep with images of her mother falling over and over again. And each time her mother fell, she got right back up.

One day after school, Ariana's feet simply started walking toward the bus that went to the rink instead of heading to the library. She had no intention of skating or talking to anyone. She just needed to breathe in the frosty air and hear the scratch of the blades again.

Sneaking into the rink was easy. Ariana knew every nook and cranny. She found a spot off to the side where no one would see her. She was like a ghost. As she hid in the shadows, she realized that it felt good just to watch. She'd rarely just watched the other girls without comparing herself to them. She stood and simply marveled at how Jenny made her arabesque look so graceful and how Sasha managed to stay so still during her spins. She watched with new eyes.

The elite girls were all out there. So was Coach Carly with her furrowed brow. She looked small against the backdrop of the arena. Ariana felt something throb in her chest.

She missed gliding on the ice but also the feeling

of being a part of something bigger than herself. Being a part of a team.

A small voice interrupted her thoughts. "Hello?"

Startled, Ariana looked toward the direction of the voice. "Who's there?" she whispered. She felt like she was trespassing and didn't want anyone to see her.

A young girl, maybe seven years old, peeked out from behind the bleachers. Dark curls jutted out from her head at strange angles. "You're Ariana, right?"

Ariana nodded.

"I come here and watch you before my own practices sometimes," the girl said.

"Oh," said Ariana. "Hey there."

The girl continued her cheerful jabbering. "You're totally my favorite skater," she said. "Probably in the whole, entire world."

When the girl grinned, Ariana saw that her two front teeth were missing. "Thanks, I guess," said Ariana. "But I don't skate anymore."

The girl's eyes got big. "Since when?"

"Well, it's a long story. But . . . " Ariana thought of holding back but heard the words spill from her mouth in a rush. "Well, I qualified for Worlds, but, well, we just don't have the money right now for me to go."

There was a long pause before the girl said, "Wow."

"I guess you could say that," said Ariana.

"Money sucks," said the girl.

"You could say that too." Ariana liked the little girl and her bluntness.

"We don't have a lot of money either, so we can't afford a lot of ice time," said the girl. "But if I were as good as you, I would *never* quit."

A tall woman with curly black hair only slightly tamer than the little girl's was suddenly standing at the end of the row of seats. "Daisy!" she said. "C'mon! It's time to get laced up."

"Wait!" said Ariana. "Your name is Daisy? You know that was my mom's — "

"Totally," said Daisy. "My mom says it's a big name to live up to when you're a little skater. But I guess you *would* know." Daisy's grin took over her entire face.

"I better get going," Daisy said. "But please don't stop skating. I'd really, *really* miss watching you."

Daisy ran toward her mother. Halfway there she stopped suddenly and stooped to the ground. A piece of metal flashed in her fingers. "Did you drop this?" she said. In her hand was Ariana's mother's necklace, whole and perfect.

Ariana was stunned. "Uh . . . yeah."

Daisy walked over and placed the necklace in Ariana's open palm.

Ariana couldn't believe that the necklace had made its way back to her. It was as if her mother was out there, somewhere, still looking out for her.

As she rolled the twirling skater around and around between her fingers, she couldn't help but think that the weight of the metal felt as light as a secret.

CHAPTER SEVEN

Ariana knew exactly what she was going to do to get to Worlds.

She was nervous. Since talking to Daisy at the rink, and finding her lost necklace, it was as if her eyes had been wiped clear. She could see now, and she knew how horrible she'd been. She'd been letting everyone down, including herself. And that wasn't like her.

She also realized that, no matter what, nothing could keep her away from skating. It may have started out as her parents' dream, but now it was hers, too.

The morning after her talk with little Daisy, Ariana threw on her signature gold hoodie, the one that clashed delightfully with her bright red hair. Instantly, she felt more like herself.

"I haven't seen that ugly old sweatshirt around here in weeks," her dad said. His eyes sparkled as he said it.

"Yeah, Dad, I'm feeling . . . better." She grabbed the piece of peanut butter toast he had made for her and gulped down some orange juice. "And I don't want you to worry. I think I have an idea of how we're going to get to Worlds."

"What kind of idea do you have?"

"Well, I think . . . " She paused because she was nervous about what he would say. "I think I want to put on a skating show." The words started to pour out of her. "And we would all perform our routines, and we would charge money." She looked at him, anxiously waiting to see what he thought.

"That sounds like an interesting plan," he said. "Well, you're going to need to reserve the arena and get tickets printed, and of course, the money will benefit the entire team."

"Of course," Ariana said.

He continued to rattle off ideas while she got out a pen and paper and started writing things down.

Ariana was thrilled that he thought that putting on a skating show would work.

They had been so absorbed in talking about the show that Ariana realized suddenly that she was going to miss her bus.

"I gotta get to the rink, Dad," she said, grabbing her bag. The peanut butter stuck in her throat, but her heart was full of hope.

Ariana stood next to Sasha's locker at the rink. She couldn't tell if she was shivering from the cold or from her nerves.

Sasha walked in. "Oh," said Sasha. "You're back." She opened her locker and tossed her bag in a little harder than necessary. Turning away from Ariana, she pulled her thick blond hair up into a high ponytail, avoiding Ariana's eyes.

"Yeah, I had some . . . things to work through," Ariana said, fiddling with the edge of her gold practice leotard.

"Oh," Sasha said. She started yanking on the strings of her skates.

Ariana tried again. "And, actually, I wanted to talk to you about something. Something you might be able to help me out with."

Sasha whipped around, her cheeks bright pink with anger. "Help you?" she said. "Why would *you* need help, Ari? Aren't you doing pretty great all by yourself?"

"I'm sorry, Sasha," said Ariana. "I was feeling . . . well, honestly? I was feeling jealous of you."

Sasha looked incredulous. "Jealous? Why would you be jealous of me? You win everything, Ari. You're the only one of us who has even the tiniest chance of going to the Olympics."

"Sasha, you have a family. An entire family. And you don't have to live up to this impossible standard. My mom was everyone's favorite. And I am *not* her, even though everyone wants me to be." It felt so good to say everything that she'd been thinking for so long.

Sasha slowly sat down on the wooden bench behind her as she listened to Ariana.

"And you were right," Ariana continued. "We have some money issues."

Sasha seemed surprised but still cool, which made Ariana nervous about sharing such personal details.

Ariana sat down next to Sasha. "I won't be able to go to Worlds at all," she said. "That is, unless my plan somehow works. And I need your help." She grabbed Sasha's hands.

"I still don't see how I can help you," Sasha said and slipped her hands out from Ariana's, smoothing invisible wrinkles on her dress. She still looked hurt.

Ariana realized then just how she had made Sasha feel. And she felt ashamed that she'd been so focused on herself and her own jealousy.

"I won't be able to do it without you, Sasha." Ariana said, reaching for Sasha's hands again. "Please hear my plan and then decide?"

Sasha looked at her for a long moment and didn't pull her hands away. "Okay. Tell me about it."

So Ariana did.

By the time she was done explaining, a few of the other girls had come into the locker room and started making suggestions. Many asked if they could be a part of the show.

Jenny came in last and stood there listening for a while, arms crossed, before she eventually stomped away. The locker room door slammed shut.

Sasha got up to follow after Jenny but met Ariana's eyes before she left and mouthed, "I'm sorry."

Ariana couldn't blame Sasha for going after Jenny. She couldn't even blame Jenny, if she thought about it.

The rest of the girls were talking all at once when Coach Carly entered the locker room. "What's going on in here?" she said. The locker room went silent at once.

Ariana met Coach Carly's eyes and remembered that she had another person that she needed to apologize to. She broke off from the pack of girls and made her way over, her head hung low.

"You're back," said Coach Carly flatly.

"Yes," said Ariana. "And I . . . I want to say sorry for how I behaved." Ariana looked up and met her coach's eyes. While she knew that her dad would feel embarrassed, she also knew that she needed to let Carly know a part of the reason she had been acting the way she had.

Sensing the need for privacy, Coach Carly hollered, "All right girls, hit the ice!" The girls filed out past them, the light-heartedness of a few moments before trailing after them.

Soon, Coach Carly and Ariana were alone.

"I need to tell you something else," Ariana said, deciding right then what she needed to say. She took a deep breath in and let the words out in a rush. "I don't have the money right now to go to Worlds. My savings — well, it's all gone."

The weight of the secret fell off of her shoulders and landed like a wet towel on the locker room floor.

Carly reached over and tucked Ariana into a tight hug. "Oh Ari," she cried. "You should have told me earlier. We could have tried to figure something out."

"I know," Ariana said. "But Dad wanted to see if he could find a better job, and he was embarrassed." Her voice dropped to a whisper. "And I couldn't stand to let you down. You've worked so hard to get me here."

"Don't you see?" said Coach Carly, throwing her arms into the air, "It's all of *your* hard work that got you here!"

"And I know you compare yourself to your mom," Coach Carly said. "Too much."

Ariana nodded.

"But you aren't her," Coach Carly said. "You don't have to be her, Ariana."

Nobody had ever said those words to her before. Ariana couldn't believe what a relief it was to hear them. She leaned into her coach again, wishing she could change how she had acted.

Carly pulled back, smiled at her, and then said, "You know what? We are going to figure something out! We can do a car wash or — "

Ariana interrupted her. "I think I have an idea," she said. "But I'm going to need your help."

CHAPTER EIGHT

"I'm going to help you, Ari," Coach Carly said after she heard Ariana's plan. "On one condition."

Ariana couldn't help but feel a small stab of worry.

"You'll need to put in extra practices after missing all of last week." Coach Carly picked Ariana's skates off the floor and pressed them to Ariana's chest. "I guess we'll see if you have what it takes."

"I do," Ariana said. "And I'll practice extra." Joy filled her body with warmth like the sun had finally decided to show her its face. She gave her coach one last quick hug. She would work as hard as she needed to. She couldn't wait to get started.

Her coach wasn't finished. "And you're only invited back if you can show me that you can be the same wonderful teammate that you had been until just recently."

Ariana felt ashamed of her behavior and of how she had talked to her friends and of how she had generally treated everyone. "I will, Coach," said Ariana. "I promise."

Ariana laced her skates up and hit the ice. At first she felt awkward. A week was the longest time she had ever been away from skating since she was five years old. Even the simplest of moves felt off-kilter.

She slipped and tripped over and over for most of the first hour, her skates feeling like they belonged to some other skater. But soon enough her muscles regained their old rhythm, and she felt like she was coming back into her body.

She started out easy with spins and footwork. When she worked in a single axel, a single toe loop, and then a double toe loop, it was as if the world had its color back. She could see the golds shining from the bleachers and the bright purple of Sasha's skirt as she circled the rink.

Sasha met her eyes once when they passed each other, giving her a small smile. Ariana guessed that Sasha still felt loyal to Jenny. Ariana also guessed that Jenny probably realized that Ariana was determined to keep her spot on the team.

Though she felt sympathy for Jenny, Ariana reminded herself that she'd earned that spot, and she was going to keep it.

As Ariana skated, she also tried to remember all of the things she had noticed while she had been watching the girls practice from the stands. She wanted to be a better teammate. She had realized that each girl had her own skill, and that maybe they could learn from each other.

Ariana skated up to Sasha. "Hey, Sasha," she said.

Sasha looked a little startled.

"I was just wondering . . . what am I doing wrong with my spins? You never move even a millimeter from your starting position."

Sasha hesitated for a long moment. "Okay," she said. "I guess let me see your spin?" She skated backward to watch.

Ariana got into position. "Here goes," she said. She skated forward and jumped into her camel spin, switching to a layback. By the time she was done, she had traveled about a foot from her starting position.

"I think I know what you're doing wrong," said Sasha. "Here. Let me show you." Sasha grabbed hold of Ariana's shoulders and repositioned her. "Now try to keep your hips more level."

The girls worked on Ariana's technique, and after about ten tries, Ariana was able to contain her spin — the movement of her skate blade across the ice — to about two inches in diameter.

"Better!" Sasha yelled.

"Thank you," said Ariana. "Coach explains it to me over and over, but hearing it come from you really made a difference."

Sasha's eyes twinkled. "You're welcome. Now let's talk about that triple axel . . ."

Ariana showed Sasha the trick of jumping farther out, instead of up, which had been the key to her getting enough spin to get around. As she talked Sasha through it, Ariana caught a glimpse of Coach Carly on the sidelines, watching the girls intently.

After a failed attempt at the triple axel and a wild landing, Sasha and Ariana burst out laughing as Sasha made a crazy face.

That night at home, Ariana was exhausted. Her entire body felt like it'd been wrung out like a rag. But she still had to get started with planning the show, so she began to make lists, trying to not yawn.

She made lists of people she would need to call. Lists of things she would need to gather. Lists of friends from school. Lists of teachers. Lists of anyone who might be able to give her a helping hand with the show. She hoped that people would be encouraged to help if they knew what they would be contributing to. Which was, Ariana thought, a dream.

Over the next few days, it was as if every door started opening for her. Everyone she asked was thrilled to pitch in. Teachers, coaches, the rink managers. Everyone except for Jenny's parents.

Ariana knew that Jenny wasn't speaking to her, so she tried to reach out to Jenny's mom and dad. They refused to answer any of Ariana's calls. She tried not to feel nervous about it even though Jenny's parents held great power at the rink due to all of the money they donated.

After the first week, the toll of double practices and organizing the show began to wear on Ariana.

Every night, she dragged her body up to bed, her eyes beginning to close before she even managed to take off her shoes. One morning her dad noticed the dark circles under her eyes.

"Hey there, Ari-girl," he said. "You need to slow down, or you aren't going to have enough energy to land even a puny single axel at Worlds. Why don't you take a breather on the show a bit?"

"I can't, Dad," Ariana said. "I'm not going to let anyone down this time."

Her dad didn't look happy, but he didn't make her stop, either. So she continued to go to school, skate double practices, and work on the show. The exhaustion began to affect her skating.

One day, five days before the show, Coach Carly pulled her aside. "You're missing your marks, Ari," said Coach Carly. "Your footwork is falling apart."

"I know," said Ariana. "I'm just so tired. I can rest for a bit after the show this weekend."

Coach Carly's face crinkled with worry. "Let's cut you back to your normal practices until then, okay?"

Ariana could have kissed her, but she was too busy skating toward the locker room, and then rushing home, and then falling into her bed.

CHAPTER NINE

Ariana's plan was slowly becoming a reality. The girls would showcase their routines at the local skating arena, inviting the entire town, and charge admission. Their goal would be to raise money for the whole team to go to Junior Worlds. Skaters other than Ariana also had parents who worked more than one or two jobs so that their girls could train and skate. Most everyone could use the help.

The skaters got permission from their skating clubs, their coaches, and the arena. They sent out flyers and advertisements. They made calls and even got some local businesses to sponsor them.

Most of all, they practiced their routines tirelessly, and they bonded as a team more than they ever had. Except for Jenny, who continued to skate by herself.

Ariana saw Jenny's mom in the stands every practice and then afterwards, talking in heated discussions with Coach Carly.

All of the other parents made sure that Ariana knew how excited they were. The day before the show, Sasha's mom pulled Ariana aside and told her how proud she was of her. "The show is going to help everyone, Ari," said Mrs. Roland. "What a great idea you had!" She squeezed Ariana's shoulder.

Ariana loved Mrs. Roland. But sometimes talking with her caused a small twinge of sadness. She would have given anything to have just one conversation with her own mom.

Excited shouts and high-fives followed the girls around school the entire week before the show, which the girls named "Skating To Worlds."

It seemed like the entire town could turn up.

Ariana couldn't help but feel nervous that something would go wrong and everyone would be disappointed in her.

Mr. Kopel promised to bring his wife and teenage kids. "We'll all be wearing gold, Ariana. Gold facepaint and everything — we'll be like your own personal statues," he said to her as she left math class, chuckling at his own joke.

"Face paint?" she said, giggling, trying to picture it.

"Yup," he said, grinning. "Even Mrs. Kopel."

Sometimes she forgot that her skating was important to other people, too. She thought about how her mom had felt all those years ago, skating on a larger stage than Ariana could even imagine.

On the Friday evening before the show, the phone rang at Ariana's house. Ariana answered. The voice on the other end sounded miserable.

"I'm afraid I have some bad news," said Coach Carly. "It looks like Jenny's parents have decided to pull their funding from the arena if we hold the show there tonight. I didn't think they'd really do it, which is why I didn't mention the threat earlier. I know how much work you've done."

Ariana's heart sank. "Why would they do that?" Ariana said, though she knew exactly why. If Ariana couldn't afford to go, Jenny would be able to take her place on the team.

She'd wondered if Jenny's parents had been planning something like this. Apparently they'd do anything to get their daughter to Worlds, including letting everyone else down.

"I'm sorry, Ariana," Coach Carly said. "I don't think that there's anything we can do. The rink relies so heavily upon her family's donations."

"But people bought tickets!" said Ariana. "What will we do?"

"I think we have to call off the show," Carly said, her voice small. "We'll just have to figure out another way to get you there."

The two of them hung up, and Ariana began to cry.

Her dad walked into the kitchen. "Why are you crying?" he asked.

"The show is off," Ariana said. She clutched her mom's necklace in her hand, wishing for once that it held some real magic.

"What?" her dad said. "Why?"

Ariana explained.

Her dad sat down with a sad look on his face. "I'm so sorry, Ari. I know how important this was to you."

"Everyone will think I screwed it up," Ariana said. The show was falling apart like she'd worried it might.

"Listen, Ari," said her father. "I've been worried about you working so hard. You're only thirteen years old. It isn't your job to be everything for everyone. Sometimes it's just your job to be thirteen."

"I know, Dad," Ariana said, brushing away tears as they rolled without permission down her cheeks. "I also know that you worked so hard for so long for me to follow this dream. This was supposed to be a way for me to help myself. And others."

"There must be something we can do," her dad said, putting his arm around her.

"Actually," he said, a grin suddenly stretching across his face. "I think I have an idea." He stood up and started to pace the kitchen back and forth with long strides. "What if the show was held at the *outdoor* rink?" he said.

"But there's not enough seating," said Ariana. "And the lights . . . We could never pull all that stuff off by tomorrow night, right?"

Ariana's dad rubbed his chin. "It'd certainly be tough to do," he said. "But I have a couple connections at the outdoor rink. And if I got a bunch of the construction guys together . . ."

Ariana looked into her dad's eyes to see a light burning there she hadn't seen in weeks. "Well," she said. "We might as well look into it."

"I can do this, Ari," said her dad. "I'd love to try to help make things right."

Ariana felt a small bubble of hope rise in her chest. The two of them began to make phone calls.

That evening, after spending the day trying to salvage the show, Ariana happily sunk into the couch. Her dad had rallied his construction friends to ready the bleachers, lights, and ice at the outdoor rink. Once again, people had come together to make the Skating to Worlds show happen. Ariana felt grateful but knew there was still a lot of work to be done the next day.

Her dad had just started dinner when Ariana heard a soft knock at the door. She went to answer it and was shocked to see who was standing outside.

"Hi, Ari," Jenny said. Her face was red and puffy like she'd been crying. She tugged nervously at the collar of her coat.

Ariana stood frozen in place like an ice sculpture.

Jenny continued, "Listen, I just wanted to say how sorry I am about what my parents did." The words rushed out quickly as if she would soon lose her courage. "I tried to stop them, but . . ." Jenny paused and raised both of her hands in a hopeless gesture. "I convinced my brother to drive me over here so I could say something, though I don't know quite what to say. But I had to do something."

"Believe me," said Ari. "I understand."

Jenny stared down at her feet, looking defeated. She said, "I have to get going," she motioned to her brother's car, idling in the driveway, "but I wanted to say good luck tomorrow, too." There was a pause as Jenny weighed her next words. "And at Worlds. You really deserve to go."

Ariana had gained her composure. "I do deserve it," she said, meaning it.

Jenny's eyes began to swim with tears.

And then, in a gentler voice, Ari continued, "I mean, I've worked as hard for this as anyone else. And so has my dad. But I also understand that this is your last chance. I'm sorry that you aren't going, because you deserved it, too."

"Yeah," Jenny said.

The silence stretched out between the girls. Finally, Jenny lifted a hand in a half-hearted wave and turned to escape into her brother's car.

CHAPTER TEN

The next day Ariana knocked at the door of Sasha's house. The girls had decided to meet there to get dressed before heading over to the outdoor rink. When Sasha greeted her with a hug, Ariana felt grateful that they were friends again.

"I wanted to show you something," Sasha said. Her body was blocking the entryway of her living room.

"Okaaay," Ariana said slowly.

Sasha made a show of pulling Ariana inside the house.

And there stood her entire team. They were dressed in brand-new skating costumes.

A colorful variety of sequins showered the room with a rainbow of shine. Their hair was stylishly piled on top of their heads. They were smiling. Great, big, happy smiles.

"Someone bought us new skating outfits," Sasha said. "And here's yours!" She held out a metallic golden dress that shimmered. The bottom edge of the skirt was delicately scalloped like the petals of a flower, and the top was shaped in a heart. Ariana could just imagine her necklace sitting perfectly in the dip. It was the most beautiful costume that she had ever seen.

Ariana looked up and was stunned to see Jenny standing there. She was standing off to the side, wearing a blue dress that matched the sparkle in her eyes.

Jenny stepped forward, looking shy. "I would love to be a part of the show, Ari . . . if you'll have me."

"Of course," Ariana managed to squeak out.

Jenny looked like maybe she was trying to shrug off the coat of sadness a bit and move on. Ariana hoped that she could. The vision of her entire team together put a huge lump in her throat.

"All right," Sasha said. "Let's get you ready!"

And then the entire team descended on Ariana, hairbrushes aloft.

The parking lot was full when Ariana and her dad drove up to the outdoor skating rink. A gentle snow had started to fall. The trees that lined portions of the rink were wrapped in colorful strands of lights. Everyone's hard work had paid off. It was like stepping into a winter dream.

A large crowd milled around the wooden entrance that had been constructed just that afternoon. Ariana could see Mr. Kopel taking tickets. He looked up and saw Ariana and waved at her with his whole arm. As promised, his face was painted a bright shiny gold.

Ariana couldn't help but laugh out loud. *I can't believe we actually pulled this off,* Ariana thought. She had never seen that many people lined up anywhere to buy tickets before.

Before Ariana knew it, it was time for the show to begin.

While the girls skated, their costumes exploded in color on the ice and gave them the appearance of dancing ice fairies. The falling snow made it feel as if the universe had joined in to make the outdoor arena into a sort of magical kingdom.

After each girl's performance, the crowd cheered and flowers rained down from all sides, just like in the big competitions. Ariana had felt like her mom was right there orchestrating the whole thing.

Before Jenny's turn on the ice, Ariana caught her eye, and the two girls smiled sadly at one another. Jenny went on to skate as if it were her last performance, each turn and jump precise and perfect, each landing punctuated with the delighted gasps of the audience. When Jenny finally bowed her last bow, tears mixed with the snowflakes dusting her cheeks.

And then it was Ariana's turn to skate.

Ariana stood alone on the ice, her left arm raised in a graceful arc above her head. Her chin tilted down. She thought of all of the people who had helped her get to that spot: Coach Carly, her teammates, Sasha's family, Mr. Kopel, and even little Daisy for helping her remember why she was out there in the first place.

Then she thought about her dad. She didn't have to look up in the stands to see if he was out there. She knew he was.

Despite the cold air, sweat pooled in the palms of her hands. Her mom's necklace was tucked down the front of her costume, and she could feel the warm metal resting against her rapidly beating heart. Her mom was right there with her. She would give it all to the ice.

Ariana's opening moves started slowly and elegantly. She danced through the first portion of her program, following every beat of the music, her nerves taking their toll with a bobble or two. She traveled a bit more with her spin combination than she would've liked, and she didn't turn her feet out enough with the layback. But she wasn't thinking about any of that. She had only one goal now.

The triple axel.

She turned the last corner, hopping, turning, leaping. And then crosscuts, backward, forward. She was picking up speed. Maybe too much.

The spot where she would either fail or succeed narrowed to one patch of ice. It loomed in the distance like a giant X on the ground. She couldn't help but think that thirteen years had been way too long to wait to get to that moment.

It was as if she had been born for it. Her heart thrummed like a hummingbird's wings.

All eyes were on her.

She skated on one leg, the next. Her thigh muscles contracted. Her blood drummed a steady rhythm in her ears. Every tiny fiber in her body seemed to work together in perfect synchronization. She could feel her feet firmly planted in her skates like they were an extension of her.

The crowd held its breath. Ariana reached the point of no return and strongly held her checked position, the leg attached to the ice bent, her free leg straight behind her. Her arms were in an L. Her form was perfect. Her body was ready. Her mind was ready. She swung her right leg up in front of her and turned.

This one's for you, Mom.

And in that moment, Ariana Gold flew.

AUTHOR BIO

Joelle Wisler is a freelance writer and physical therapist who specializes in working with athletes of all ages. She is a life-long runner, jumper, bender, and skier and now specializes in chasing kids and any stray moose that might wander into her Colorado mountain backyard. Once upon a time, Joelle's sports dream was to be six feet tall so that she could dunk a basketball, but stopping at five-foot-two made her realize that she'd have to settle for just being fast. She writes about kids and motherhood at the *Huffington Post*, on her blog, and at other online publications.